Helen Orme taught for many years before giving up teaching to write full-time. At the last count she had written over 70 books.

She writes both fiction and non-fiction, but at present is concentrating on fiction for older readers.

Helen also runs writing workshops for children and courses for teachers in both primary and secondary schools.

How many have you read?

Moving

Helen Orme

Ransom

Moving

by Helen Orme
Illustrated by Cathy Brett
Cover by Anna Torborg

Published by Ransom Publishing Ltd.
51 Southgate Street, Winchester, Hants. SO23 9EH
www.ransom.co.uk

ISBN   978 184167 689 0

First published in 2007

Meet the Sisters ...

Siti and her friends are really close. So close she calls them her Sisters. They've been mates for ever, and most of the time they are closer than her real family.

Siti is the leader – the one who always knows what to do – but Kelly, Lu, Donna and Rachel have their own lives to lead as well.

Still, there's no one you can talk to, no one you can rely on, like your best mates. Right?

1

Two lots of news

Donna was early at school on Monday morning. She wanted to share her news with her friends.

Siti was the first one in.

"Guess what!" said Donna. "Marie's got a new job."

Marie was Donna's older sister.

"Why is that so exciting?" asked Siti.

"She's working for the Gazette. She's going to do secretarial work and get a chance to do some reporting."

"Kelly is going to be so jealous," said Siti. "You know she wants to be a writer."

Kelly and Rachel were both excited when Donna told them the news. But Lu didn't seem that interested.

"What's up?" Siti asked Lu later.

"Oh," she sighed. "It's my mum and dad again."

"What is it this time?"

Siti liked Lu's parents, but she knew that they were always getting ideas about things Lu should be doing. Sometimes the ideas were good ones, but sometimes they were a disaster!

"It's school," sighed Lu.

"What's the matter with school?" said Siti. Her dad was a teacher at their school and she could get a bit funny if people said rude things about the place.

"They think I need to work harder!"

"There's better things to do in school than work hard," laughed Donna.

"No, this is serious – not just parents being parents. They want to send me to St. Joan's!"

2

"This is serious!"

"But they can't take you away from here," said Kelly.

"They said that I need really good grades in my exams," Lu said.

"But it's years 'til then," said Rachel.

"I've got to have time to 'settle in'!"

They all knew about St. Joan's. It was a girl's school on the other side of town. They made the girls wear uniforms – with hats!

Siti and Kelly were talking about it later.

"You know what Lu's mum and dad are like," said Siti. "They don't think that this place is good enough for Lu."

"Yeah, they are a bit snobby," agreed Kelly. "They are always trying to get her to do things she doesn't want to do."

"But this is serious," said Siti. "We've got to get them to change their minds."

"Why don't you talk to your dad?" said Kelly. "He might help."

So, at home that evening, Siti talked to her dad.

"Well," he said, "I can understand why Lu's mum and dad want the best for Lu."

"But is it the best?" asked Siti.

"I don't think so," said Dad, "but they do get very good exam results."

"Oh, bother exam results," said Siti. "What can we do NOW?"

"Well, sit down with Lu and make a list of the reasons why she should stay with us. But she needs to talk to her mum and dad herself. Be careful about your bright ideas!"

Siti laughed. The last time they had had a bright idea to help Lu, it had nearly turned into a disaster.

3

St. Joan's

Next day at school, Siti told Lu what her dad had said. At lunch time they got a piece of paper and started to make a list.

At first, Rachel and Donna came up with some daft ideas.

"Sexy boys – none at St. Joan's."

"Better uniform – no stupid hats."

"Come on! Be serious," said Siti. "We've got to find good reasons."

"Well, we do lots of charity things – that's good."

"The exam results are O.K. – I don't know what my mum and dad are moaning about really."

"What else is good?" said Siti. "I haven't got a very long list yet."

"How about writing all the bad things about St. Joan's?"

By the time lunch break was over they had made two lists. But, as Siti said, they weren't much help.

"We're going to have to do better than this," she said.

That night, Lu tried to talk to her parents.

"I'm sorry," said her dad. "But we've made up our minds."

"We're all going to visit the school next week," said her mum.

Whatever Lu said, they just would not listen. In the end, she stormed out of the room and stamped off upstairs to her bedroom.

The visit to the school was just what Lu expected. She told the Sisters all about it the next day.

"The girls were all snobby, the uniform is manky, the teachers look as if they never have a laugh and the buildings look as if they're falling down."

"What did your mum and dad think?" asked Siti.

"They just talked to the Head. They thought she was wonderful. It's no good, it's all sorted. I'm starting there next term."

4

"We've got to think of something"

Lu was really, really upset. So were the rest of the Sisters. They didn't want her to leave.

"It won't be the same without Lu," said Rachel.

"We've got to think of something," said Kelly.

They thought of loads of ideas.

"Lock yourself in your bedroom until they agree to listen to you."

"Work harder – do more homework."

"Tell them it costs too much."

Whatever they suggested, Lu said it was no good.

Siti tried talking to her dad again.

"Can't you do something? Can't the Head?"

"We can't tell parents what to do. You know that," he said.

In the end, he got fed up with Siti going on.

"You are just going to have to leave it, Siti," he said. "There's nothing *you* can do, there's nothing *I* can do."

But Siti wasn't going to leave it. She hated seeing Lu so unhappy.

She thought about what Lu had said about St. Joan's. It didn't sound like a good school. Their own school was a nice building with teachers who looked happy and who cared.

"Well, they all care, except Dad!" she thought.

Then she had an idea. What about asking some of the other teachers for ideas? Who would be best? Which teachers really liked Lu?

5

Miss Drake has a think

Siti and Lu went to talk to Miss Drake. Siti explained the problem.

"I don't want to go," said Lu. "I want to stay here. This is a good school. St. Joan's looked horrible."

Miss Drake listened to them carefully.

"Well," she said, "I knew you were leaving, but I didn't know you felt so strongly about it. But I don't see how I can help."

"I've thought about it," said Siti. "You could tell Mr and Mrs Clarke that St. Joan's is no good and that Lu would be better here."

Miss Drake looked uncomfortable. "Why do you think it's no good?" she asked.

Lu repeated all the things she'd told the Sisters.

Siti was watching Miss Drake's face. "She knows something," she thought. "I wonder what it is?"

"I'll have a think," Miss Drake told them. "But I can't make any promises!"

Later that day, Miss Drake went to talk to Siti's dad.

"She's a clever girl, your daughter," she said.

"Why?"

"Because she's picked up that there's trouble at St. Joan's."

"What sort of trouble?"

"Well, my friend Fran works there. The staff didn't get paid last month. The Head says it will all be sorted soon, but Fran's really worried. And she's not the only one!"

That gave Mr Musa a lot to think about.

He spoke to Siti that night. "Have Lu's mum and dad paid anything yet?" he asked.

"Don't know – why?"

"Well, you mustn't tell anybody but …" and he told Siti what Miss Drake had said.

Siti thought about it all night. She had to tell the Sisters. Something must be done!

6

Scandal!

Next day, she told them everything she knew. "We've got to find out more," she said.

"I need to stop my mum and dad paying out," said Lu. "They're going to send a cheque next week."

"How do we find out what's going on?" asked Kelly.

"Marie!" said Donna. "She can talk to people at work."

"She'd better do it quickly then," said Lu.

Later, when she thought about it all, Siti was surprised just how quickly everything had happened.

A few days later, Donna rang Lu.

"Marie says you've got to look at the Gazette tomorrow."

"Why?"

"She wouldn't tell me. She says it's secret until the paper comes out. Just go and buy it."

The next day, on the way home, Lu bought the newspaper. She looked at the story on the front page. There was a photo of St. Joan's with a picture of the Head standing at the front door.

She read the headline.

Scandal at St. Joan's

Marie was really pleased with herself. She had told her boss and he had done some digging. They had found out what was going on.

The school had no money left. The police were looking into where it had all gone. The headteacher was 'helping with their enquiries.'

There were plans to sell the school and knock it down for houses.

Every week for the rest of term, more of the story came out. It was even on television.

It got worse and worse. The Head was arrested and the school closed. The parents were very cross because they lost the money they'd paid. The girls had no schools to go to.

Just before the end of term, Donna had another message for Lu.

"Marie says you've got to look at the Gazette tomorrow."

The headline made Lu really happy.

LOCAL COMP BEST
IN THE COUNTY

She read the story.

The exam results for the last year were so good that their school was top of the list.

She showed the paper to her parents.

"Now will you listen to me?" she said. "I told you so!"